Written by Deborah Chancellor
Illustrated by Simon Mendez (Advocate)

This edition published by Parragon in 2010

Parragon
Queen Street House
4 Queen Street
Bath BA1 1HE, UK

ISBN 978-1-4075-7848-4

Printed in China

Muddypaws
and the
Birthday Party

PaRragon
Bath · New York · Singapore · Hong Kong · Cologne · Delhi · Melbourne

Ben was just a smallish, normalish boy, but he was Muddypaws' **best friend.**

They went out for the best **splishy-splashy** muddy walks together.

They made new friends together of all sizes, colours and smells.

They did everything together.

But one sunny morning, Muddypaws woke up
to find everything had changed in his house.
There were lots of new things!

He sniffed about excitedly. What was happening?
Where was Ben? He scampered off to find him.

"WOOF!" barked Muddypaws, dropping his favourite ball at Ben's feet.

"Let's play!"

But Ben was busy playing with a strange shiny thing.
And the strange shiny thing was getting bigger ...
and bigger ... and BIGGER!

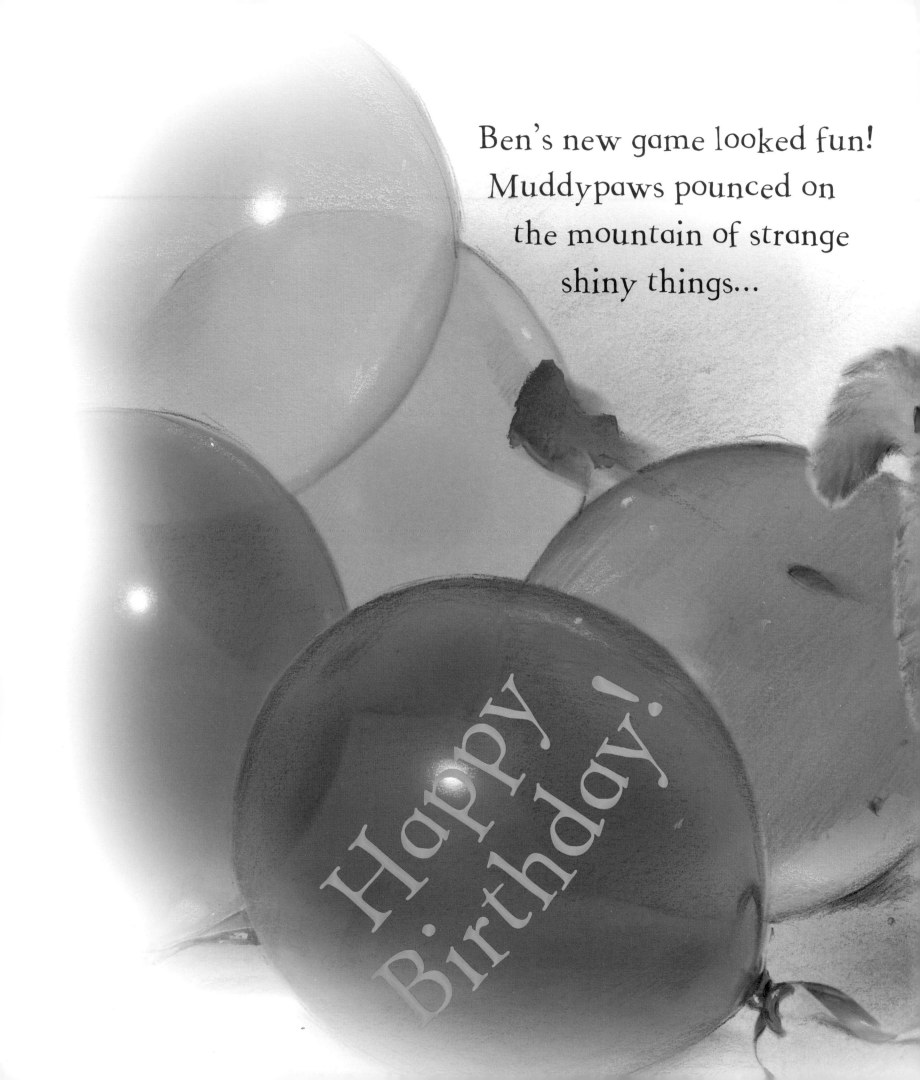

Ben's new game looked fun!
Muddypaws pounced on
the mountain of strange
shiny things...

Happy Birthday!

Bang! Muddypaws jumped away as fast as he could. He didn't like that game! But what was that delicious smell coming from the kitchen...?

His tail began to wag. **Sausages!**
Surely no one would mind...

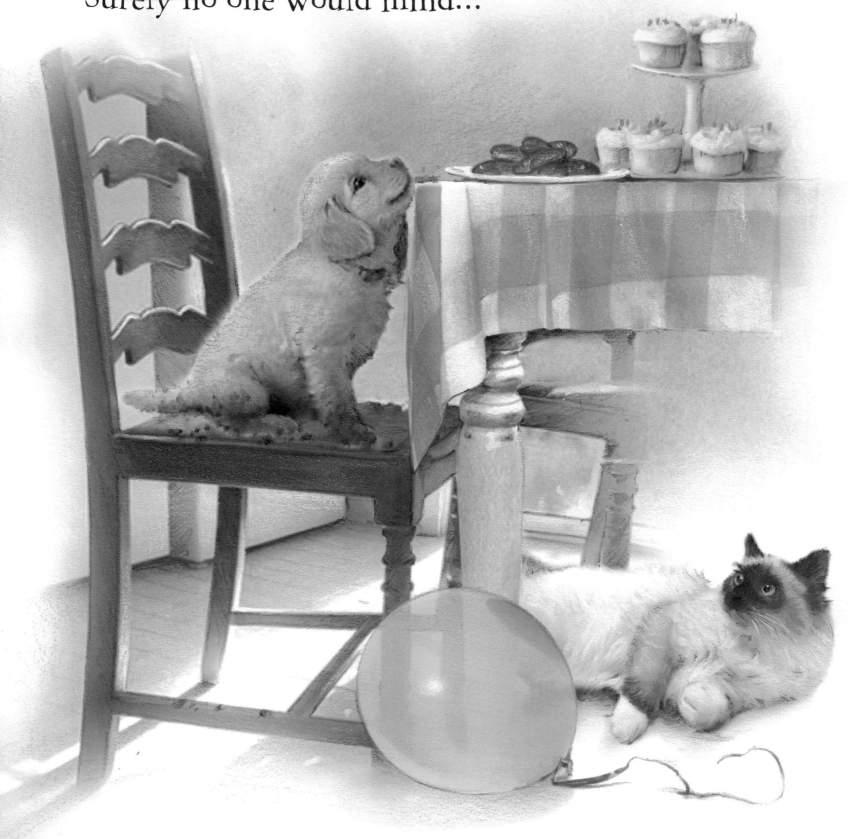

... if he tried a little one? But someone did mind!

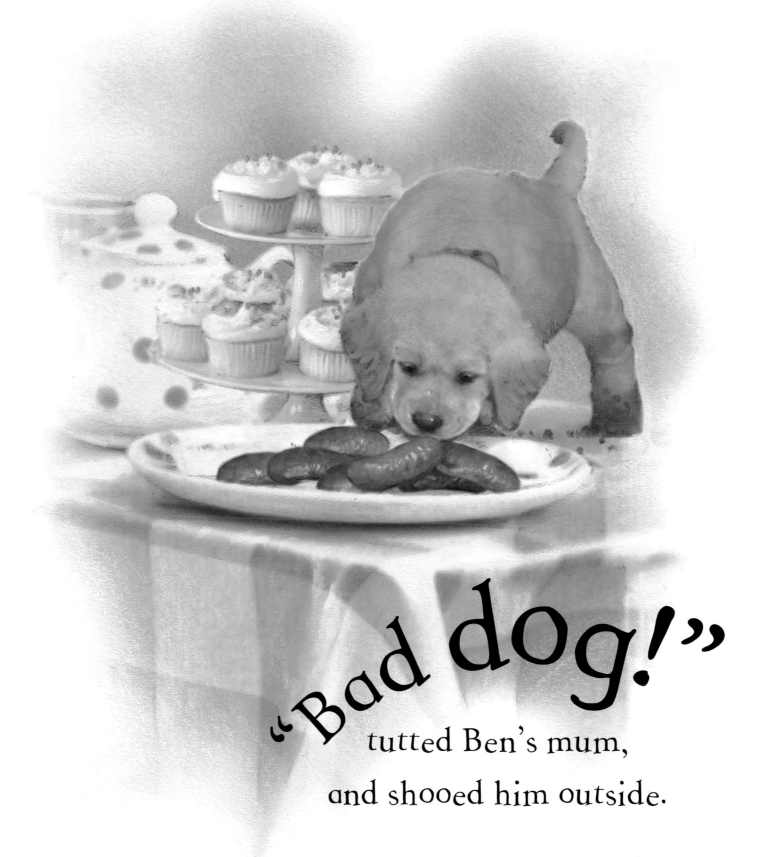

"*Bad dog!*"
tutted Ben's mum,
and shooed him outside.

Muddypaws' tail stopped wagging. Why didn't
Ben want to play with him? Why was everything
different today?

Maybe Honey the cat would want to play.
"WOOF!" barked Muddypaws. "Let's play!"
Honey turned up her nose.

She had better things to do than play with a puppy –
like rolling on the grass in the sunshine!

Then the garden gate **squeaked** open...

...and the garden was filled with stamping feet, new smells and loud voices.

A crowd of children ran up the garden path into the house.

Something interesting was certainly going on –
and Muddypaws was stuck in the garden with
no one to play with.

The flowers were **boring**. The grass was
boring. Even the smells were **boring**.
And Muddypaws was getting hungry.
He tried to find his bone...

...but it had disappeared.

What was happening inside the house? Perhaps he would just look through the window to see.

Muddypaws pushed his nose up against the glass. Ben and the other children were running around and laughing. They looked like they were having a great time!

Muddypaws wanted to join in more than anything in the **whole world**.

Then Ben's mum walked into the room carrying something that was twinkling brightly.

It was the **biggest**, most **delicious** looking cake Muddypaws had ever seen, and it was covered in little lights!

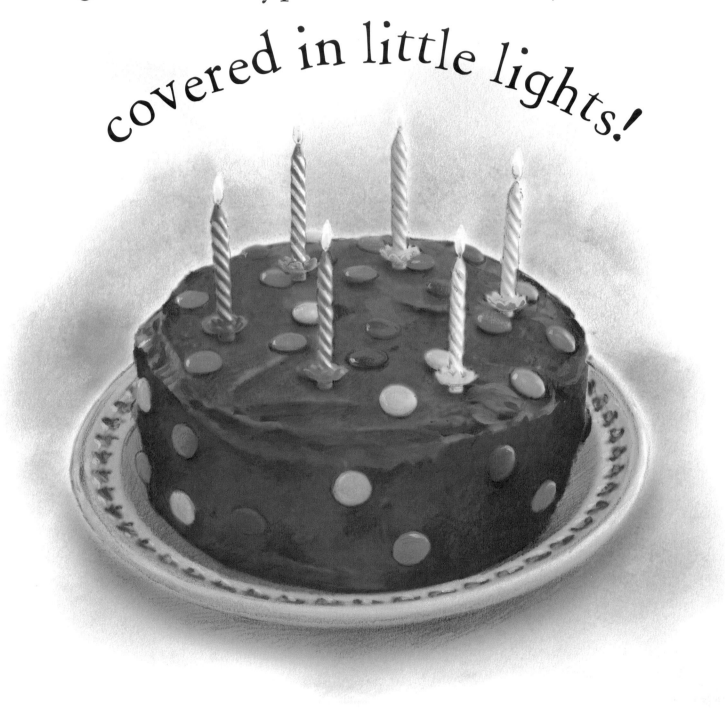

Muddypaws licked his lips and pressed his nose
even harder against the window.
Suddenly, the door opened.

It was Ben.

"Mum says you can come in now!" cried Ben.

But all at once, Muddypaws didn't want to come inside.

He didn't like the big shiny things that went **bang!**

He didn't like it when
Ben's mum shouted at him.

He wasn't sure about all the
new children in his house.

"I know what to do," Ben said.

Ben threw Muddypaws' ball high into the sky.

At once, Muddypaws forgot about
the big shiny things...
He forgot about the new children...
He even forgot about Ben's mum shouting...

Ben wanted to play with him!
Muddypaws jumped and barked for joy.
He ran as fast as he could to fetch his ball,
and brought it back to Ben.

Ben scooped Muddypaws into his arms and gave him a big hug. "I'm sorry, Muddypaws!" he whispered. "You didn't know it was my birthday. But you do know you're my best friend, don't you?"

"And best friends do everything together – especially sharing birthday treats!"

"WOOF!" barked Muddypaws.

"Sausages!"